three
amigos

The Case of the

CRYBABY COWBOY

by Carole Marsh

D1340188

Published by Gallopade International/Carole Marsh Books.
Printed in the United States of America.

Managing Editor: Sherry Moss
Cover Design: Michele Winkelman
Illustration: Cecil Anderson

Picture Credits: Carole Marsh

Gallopade is proud to be a member and supporter of these
educational organizations and associations:
American Booksellers Association
International Reading Association
National Association for Gifted Children
The National School Supply and Equipment Association
The National Council for the Social Studies
Museum Store Association
Association of Partners for Public Lands

Dedicated to the "real" Grant, Weng-Ho, and Seve.
Thank you for being such great "characters."

A Word From the Author

Dear Reader,

Maybe you wonder how writers get their ideas? I got the idea for this book by watching three boys grow up together and become good friends, best buddies—and have a great time together! I think boys are really, really good at making friends for life, supporting one another, and sticking together in good times and in bad. Also, I had just been to Cody, Wyoming to the famous Buffalo Bill Museum. While I was there, I bought a book on "brands." If you don't know what that is—you will as soon as you read this story! If this makes you interested in "cowboy brands," you might also enjoy learning about barbwire, which also has different styles for each ranch. Or, maybe I will just have to write a book about that too!

By the way, here is my brand!

About the Three Amigos

Weng-Ho, Grant, and Seve are best friends.

Weng-Ho is 7. Grant is 8. Seve is 9.

They live on the same street. Weng-Ho lives next door to Grant. Grant lives next door to Seve.

They go to the same school. Weng-Ho's classroom is next to Grant's. Grant's classroom is next to Seve's.

They each have a younger or older sister. Weng-Ho has a baby sister. Grant has an older sister. Seve has an even older sister.

They ride the school bus together. They eat lunch together. They go to recess together. Sometimes they get in trouble together. They like to solve riddles, mysteries, and puzzles together.

Or, at least they like to try!

BOOKS IN THIS SERIES

TABLE OF CONTENTS

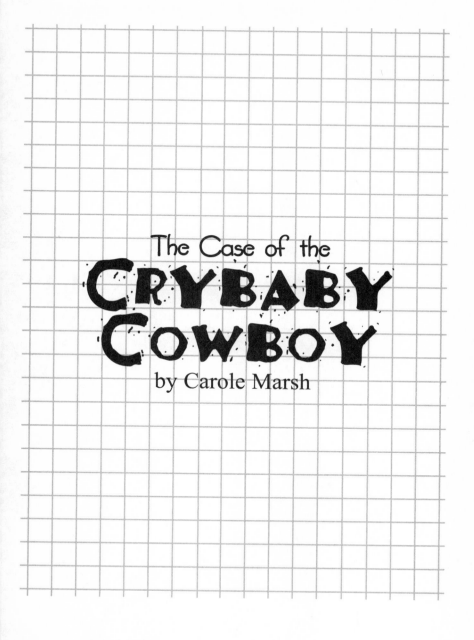

The Case of the
CRYBABY
COWBOY
by Carole Marsh

A NEW KID IN TOWN

Grant, Seve, and Weng-Ho were having breakfast together. They sat around the table in Grant's kitchen. They were chowing down on chocolate chip pancakes made by Grant's dad.

"The school bus comes in ten minutes," said Grant's dad.

Chomp! Chomp! Chomp! Chomp!

The boys chewed faster. This made Grant giggle. Then Weng-Ho giggled. Then Seve began to giggle. Soon, milk was dribbling down their chins.

Grant's mom walked into the kitchen. She was ready to go to work. She wore a suit. She wore high heel shoes. She carried a briefcase. She laughed.

"What is going on?" asked Grant's mom. "You boys are so funny. You are just like the Three Musketeers."

Grant shook his head. "No we aren't," he said. "The Three Musketeers were old guys. We are just kids."

"The Three Musketeers did not let milk dribble down their chins," said Grant's dad. "Wipe your mouths and get ready to catch the bus."

The boys wiped their faces with their napkins. They took their plates to the sink. They grabbed their jackets and backpacks and ran out the door.

Weng-Ho hopped on the school bus first. Grant hopped on second. Seve hopped on third.

"Good morning," said the driver. "Please take your seats."

"Good morning," said the boys. They ran to the back of the bus and sat on the very last seat.

"Today is Monday," said Seve. "I have a spelling test."

"I have a math test," said Weng-Ho.

"I have a reading test," said Grant. "I wish we had a mystery to solve instead."

"Maybe a mystery will come our way," said Weng-Ho. "Let's keep our eye out for a mystery."

"A Monday mystery," said Seve.

The school bus came to a stop in front of the school and the boys jumped off and ran to their classrooms.

Grant skipped into his classroom. He took his seat. He sat in the third chair in the fourth row.

"Good morning, Grant," said his teacher.

"Good morning, teacher," said Grant.

"Say hello to our new student," the teacher said.

Grant looked around. He saw a new boy sitting in the chair beside him. The boy was Grant's age. He was Grant's size.

But he was dressed very differently.

The new student wore jeans with some funny-looking leather pants over the top of them. He wore a plaid shirt with a bandanna tied around his neck. He wore cowboy boots on his feet and a cowboy hat on his head.

"Are you a cowboy?" Grant asked the new boy.

But the new boy did not answer. He looked straight ahead. Grant saw one tiny tear trickle down the new boy's cheek.

Grant was so surprised. He felt sad. Why would the new boy cry? Was he sad? He did not know what to do. He did not know what to say.

At lunch, Grant rushed to meet Seve and Weng-Ho. They always sat at the same  table together. It was the fifth table in the second row. But today, Grant had a surprise.

"I think we have a Monday mystery!" Grant said, as soon as he had sat down.

Monday was hot dog and baked beans day. The other boys began to eat while they listened to Grant.

"He is a new kid," Grant said. "He dresses like a cowboy. But he is sad. He will not talk. And he cried in class."

"That is a mystery," said Seve. "I wonder who he is? I wonder where he came from? I wonder why he is so sad?"

"Why don't you ask him?" said Weng-Ho. "He is sitting right over there."

Weng-Ho pointed to the fourth table in the fifth row. The new kid sat all by himself. He still looked sad, but he was really chowing down on his beans and hot dog.

The principal came by. He patted Grant, Weng-Ho, and Seve on their heads. "You boys are just like the Three Stooges," he said.

"No," said Grant. "The Three Stooges are very silly actors. We are just kids."

The principal laughed and walked off. The boys did not laugh. They just kept watching the Crybaby Cowboy.

That night at home, Grant told his mother about the Crybaby Cowboy.

"What do you think about him?" his mom asked, as she tucked Grant into bed.

"I think he is sad," said Grant. "And

I think he is a mystery."

"If you were sad, what would you want someone to do?" his mom asked.

"I would want someone to be nice to me," Grant said.

"And how do you solve a mystery?" Grant's mom asked.

"You have to find clues," said Grant.

Grant's mother kissed him goodnight. "Then tomorrow in school, maybe you should be nice and you will find some clues to solve your mystery."

Mysterious Markings 2

The next day at school, Grant went right to his classroom. He was late so he went right to his seat.

The teacher stood in front of the class. "As you may have noticed," she said, "we have a new student in our class."

The cowboy kid stood up. But he did not look up. He looked down at his desk. He still wore his cowboy hat, cowboy boots, jeans with the funny leather pants on top, and a different plaid shirt and bandanna. He had been crying. Grant

could see the track where a tear had slid
down his cheek.

"Please come up to the blackboard,"
the teacher told the new student.

The Crybaby Cowboy walked slowly
up to the blackboard.

"Please write your name on the
board," the teacher said.

To everyone in the classroom's
surprise, the boy took a piece of chalk and
drew this on the blackboard:

"Thank you," said the teacher. "Now write where you came from, please."

Again, to his classmate's surprise, the Crybaby Cowboy drew this on the blackboard:

"Now please write where you live today," the teacher said.

The Crybaby Cowboy picked up the

piece of chalk one last time. He wrote:

"Thank you," said the teacher. "You may sit back down."

The Crybaby Cowboy sat down. The other kids in the room all stared at him. Everyone wondered what the strange symbols meant. The boy did not explain. The teacher did not explain. The teacher just smiled a secret smile. The boy just looked sad.

SOLVING THE MYSTERY 3 three

Grant could hardly wait to get to recess to see his friends. "Hey," he said, "you won't believe what happened in class today."

He told Seve and Weng-Ho about the Crybaby Cowboy and how he had drawn strange symbols on the blackboard that no one could figure out.

Seve hung upside down on the monkey bars. "What do you think they mean?" he asked Grant.

"I don't know," said Grant.

Weng-Ho slid down the sliding board. "Well why don't you ask him?" he said. "He is right over there." Weng-Ho pointed to the swings. The Crybaby Cowboy was

 swinging all alone.

Just then the bell rang and all the kids dashed inside. Before he and Weng-Ho and Seve went inside, Grant showed them a piece of paper. "I copied the symbols down," he said. "Tonight I will ask Dad what they mean. We will solve the Case of the Crybaby Cowboy!"

That night, Grant told his dad about the symbols. He showed his father the piece of paper where he had copied down the Crybaby Cowboy's strange symbols.

"Aha!" said Grant's dad. "Do you know what these are?"

"No," said Grant, "that's why I'm asking you."

"Right," said Grant's dad. "Well, these symbols are called brands. Brands are what cowboys use to mark their cattle. If you mark your cattle with your brand, then you can tell your cattle apart from another rancher's cattle."

Grant thought about how much one cow looked like another cow. "That would be a good idea," he said.

"And," said his dad. "A brand can keep rustlers from stealing your cattle— because it has a brand on it."

"Wow!" said Grant, "are there still cattle rustlers?"

"Yes," his dad said. "The Wild West

is still pretty wild. Some people still rustle cattle if they get a chance. They can even try to change one brand to look like another. Let's see if we can figure out what these brands mean."

"I think we need help!" said Grant. "Can Weng-Ho and Seve come over and help?"

"Sure," said his dad. "Give them a call."

Soon, Grant and Seve and Weng-Ho sat around the kitchen table. Grant's dad had to go to work. But he had left them a few clues. Here are the clues he left:

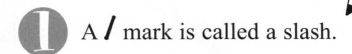

1 A **/** mark is called a slash.

2 A — mark is called a bar.

3 Many symbols look like what they mean.

"Ok," said Grant. "Let's get started.

The first symbol the Crybaby Cowboy drew on the board was his name. It looks like this:

"So your Dad's clues must mean that the Crybaby Cowboy's first name is Slash?" said Weng-Ho.

"Yes!" said Grant. "That sure is a funny name."

"Maybe not for a cowboy," said Seve.

"That's true," said Grant. "Now let's see if we can figure out his last name."

KER

"Well at least it has letters," said Seve.

"Yes," said Grant. "And it has a bar symbol over them."

"Then I think the Crybaby Cowboy's last name is BARKER!" said Seve.

"That sounds right to me," said Grant.

"Slash Barker," said Weng-Ho.

"The next thing the teacher asked the Crybaby Cowboy to draw on the board is where he came from," Grant said. "This is what he drew."

The three boys looked and looked at the symbols. They turned the symbols this way and that.

Finally, Grant said, "Let's remember Dad's clue that some brands look like what they mean."

Seve pointed to the top symbol.

"Maybe it's an igloo."

"I don't think cowboys use igloos," said Grant.

"Maybe it's a mountain," said Weng-Ho.

"It looks more like a hill than a mountain," said Seve.

"It could be a hat," said Grant. "Let's pretend for a minute that it is a hat."

The boys looked at the symbol under the hat.

"A snake?" guessed Seve.

"A crooked road?" guessed Grant.

"How about a river? Or a creek?" said Weng-Ho.

"Hat Snake? Hat Road? Hat Creek?"

said Grant.

Grant's mother walked through the kitchen. "Hat Creek?" she said. "That is a town in Wyoming. Your Dad and I went horseback riding there once."

"Yeah!" said the three boys.

"HAT CREEK! HAT CREEK, WYOMING!"

"That is where the Crybaby Cowboy came from!"

Next, the boys studied the symbols that looked like this:

45 M

"This is what the Crybaby Cowboy drew when the teacher asked where he lives now," Grant said.

"These look too hard to figure out," said Seve.

"We have to try," said Weng-Ho.

"Let's just take one at a time," said Grant.

"The first one looks like a 4," said Seve.

"No, a 5," said Grant.

"A 4 and a 5," said Weng-Ho.

"Hey, maybe it is a 4 AND a 5," said Grant. "That would be 45!"

"Like a house number?" Seve guessed.

"Yes, I think so," said Grant.

"Now for the second part," said Weng-Ho.

"Hmm, that has to be an M," said Seve.

"It sure looks like an M," said Grant.

"But what's that thing under it?" asked Weng-Ho.

"A hole?" guessed Seve.

"A U?" guessed Grant.

"How about a rocker?" said Weng-Ho.

"Hmm," said Grant. "M Hole? M U? M Rocker?"

"None of those sound right?" said Seve.

Grant's mother walked back through the kitchen. She looked over the boys' shoulders. "I think you might mean Rocking M," she said. "That is the name of a Boy's Ranch nearby."

"Wow! So the Crybaby Cowboy lives at 45 Rocking M," said Grant.

"What is a boy's ranch?" Weng-Ho asked Grant's mom.

"It is an orphanage," Grant's mom

said.

"Wow!" said Grant, "You mean where kids go when they don't have any parents?"

"That's right," Grant's mother said.

"No wonder the Crybaby Cowboy cries," said Seve sadly.

"Well, at least we solved the mystery," said Weng-Ho.

Grant shook his head. "No. I think there is more to the Case of the Crybaby Cowboy."

"Like what?" asked Seve.

"Like how to help him be not so sad," said Grant.

The next day at school, Grant ran straight to his classroom. He went right up to the Crybaby Cowboy.

"Hi," Grant said.
"I'm Grant. I'll bet
you are Slash Barker!"

The new kid looked
very surprised. "Yes I am,"
he said.

"And I'll bet you came here from Hat
Creek, Wyoming," Grant said.

The new kid looked very, very
surprised. "I sure did," he said.

"And I think you must live at 45
Rocking M now," said Grant.

"I do!" said the new kid. "But how
did you figure all that out?"

Grant smiled. "You gave us the brand
clues on the board. Then my Dad gave

some clues as to how to figure them out.
I never met a cowboy before. Would you
like to meet my friends?"

"Yes!" said the new kid.

"Yee-ha!!!"

At lunch, Grant, Seve, and Weng-Ho
invited the new kid to sit at their table.
They sat at the first table in the first row.
It was hamburger day.

"I think I have a brand on my
hamburger," said Weng-Ho.

"The brand is on the outside of the
cow," said the new kid. "Not the inside."

"What are those funny pants you wear over your jeans?" Seve asked the new kid.

"They are called chaps," said the new kid. "Cowboys wear them when they ride horses to round up cattle."

"Do you ride horses?" asked Weng-Ho.

"Of course I do," said the new kid. "I'm a cowboy!"

"But why are you so sad?" asked Grant. "Is it because you live in an orphanage?"

The new kid shook his head. "No," he said. "I like it at 45 Rocking M. Everyone is very nice to me. We have horses there. You could even come visit and ride with me."

"Then why did you cry in class?"
asked Seve.

"Because I'm still a little homesick
for Hat Creek and my school and friends
back in Wyoming."

Now all the boys looked sad. They
could understand how the new kid felt.
But then the new kid did a funny thing.

He smiled real big. "I'm not so sad now," he said to his new friends.

All of a sudden, a big mean kid came by. "Hi, there, crybaby," he snarled at the new kid.

Grant, Weng-Ho, and Seve stood up.

"Don't you call him a crybaby!" said Grant.

"Because he's not," said Seve.

"He's a cowboy!" said Weng-Ho proudly.

"Ok, ok," said the big mean kid, and he walked off.

Just then Grant's teacher walked by. "You boys sure do tickle me," she said. "You are just like…just like…just like **THREE AMIGOS!** Three best friends."

Grant, Weng-Ho, and Seve looked at one another. Then they threw their arms around each other and grinned. "We are not just like Three Amigos," said Grant. "We ARE Three Amigos!"

All the boys laughed, even the Crybaby Cowboy, who was so happy to have not one—but three—new friends that he tossed his cowboy hat into the air and yelled

"Yee-ha!!!"

And everyone in the lunchroom
clapped their hands and cheered!

Cowboy Brands

Back in the old days, there were no fences on the western prairie. The cattle roamed on "open range." To identify cattle from different ranches, brands were used.

A brand is a special mark made up of one or more letters, numbers, or picture symbols or shapes. A brand is put on a cow by burning it onto its hide with a "branding iron."

The American cowboys made up brands that were simple to remember. You can "read" a brand just by looking at it—once you learn how.

A brand is read:
From left to right
From top to bottom
From outside to inside

Brands are made up of a "cowboy
alphabet." Here are some examples of
brands or parts of brands:

A, like the letter A
12, like the number 12
O, like the shape of a circle

There are other figures in the cowboy
brand alphabet:
A ▬ is called a bar.
A ▬▬▬ is called a rail.

A diagonal shape this way **/** or this way ****
is called a slash.

A ▢ is called a box.

A ⌣ is called a rocker.

Then the cowboys did some fancy things
with their numbers, letters, and figures.

RR   ЯR   ꙅⱰ

R̥   R̩

An **R** is read R.

This **ꙅⱰ** is called a lazy R.

This **ЯƂ** is a crazy R.

Here's a flying R **Ɽ**.

Can you think of other ways to fancy up
an R?

46

When cowboys began to put their special alphabet together, they created interesting brands. Remember the "how to read a brand" rules and see if you can figure out how to say these brands:

How about these?

Here are the answers:

Circle A

Bar Box

Two X star

Slash J

X box

Lazy J

Hey, tenderfoot, get a piece of paper and make up some of your own cowboy brands!

ABOUT THE SERIES CREATOR

Carole Marsh writes lots of books for kids. She started writing when she was just a kid. She is married to a cowboy named Bob. She likes to ride horses and figure out riddles, puzzles, and mysteries. Grant is her real-life grandson. Weng-Ho and Seve are his real-life amigos!

GLOSSARY

amigo: a Spanish word for friend

bandanna: a cotton scarf worn around the neck

cattle: cows raised for their meat or milk

prairie: large areas of grassland

ranch: a large piece of land where cattle are raised

rustler: someone who tries to steal another rancher's cattle

tenderfoot: someone who is not a cowboy

TALK ABOUT IT!

Hey, Kids, Parents, Teachers!

Need some help discussing your book in your book club? Read on!

1. Who are the main characters?

2. Which character do you like best? Why?

3. What is the mystery the characters try to solve?

4. Why did you think the new student was crying?

5. Discuss how to help a new student who is lonely.

6. Why do you think the new student wrote on the chalkboard instead of talking out loud?

7. How do the boys solve the mystery?

8. What did you like or dislike about the book?

9. What one thing will you always remember about this book?

BRING IT TO LIFE!

Now that you've read *The Crybaby Cowboy,* try these suggestions in your next book club meeting!

1. Dress up like cowboys and cowgirls! Wear jeans, boots, hats, and bandannas!

2. Taste it! Get some sugar cookies and icing. Use the icing to create your own brand on a cookie!

3. Read *The Cowboy Christmas Ball* by Carole Marsh.

4. Map it Out! Bring in a big map of the United States. Find Wyoming. List all the states you would have to travel through to get from your state to Wyoming!

5. Bring in a guest speaker! Maybe your media specialist can help you find someone who knows about ranches and the Old West.

6. Take a field trip! Find a place where you can pet some horses!

7. Learn to do the "2 Step" cowboy dance.

TECH CONNECTS

Hey, Kids! Visit www.carolemarshmysteries.com to:

JOIN THE CAROLE MARSH MYSTERIES FAN CLUB!

LEARN REAL-LIFE COWBOY TRIVIA!

DOWNLOAD INFORMATION ABOUT GETTING ALONG AND MAKING NEW FRIENDS!

DOWNLOAD A BRANDING ACTIVITY!